Piglet and Mama

by Margaret Wild

illustrated by

Stephen Michael King

SCHOLASTIC INC.
New York Toronto London Auckland Sydney
Mexico City New Delhi Hong Kong Buenos Aires

For Karen & Olivia —M.W.

For Enya —S.M.K.

Stephen Michael King used watercolor and black ink for the illustrations in this book.

ISBN-13: 978-0-545-00292-9
ISBN-10: 0-545-00292-3

12 11 10 9 8 7 6 5 4 3 2 1   7 8 9 10 11/0

Printed in the U.S.A.   08
First Scholastic printing, January 2007

One morning in the farmyard,
Piglet lost her mama.

"Oiiiiiink!" cried Piglet.
So with a snuffle and a snort,
off she went to look for her mama.

"Mama!" said Piglet.

"Your mama's not here," said Duck.

"Let's have a cuddle."

But Piglet wanted her mama.

"Mama!" said Piglet.

"Your mama's not here," said Sheep.

"Let's make a daisy chain."

But Piglet wanted her mama.

"Mama!" said Piglet.

"Your mama's not here,"
said Donkey.

"Let's play chase."

But Piglet wanted her mama.

"Mama!" said Piglet.

"Your mama's not here," said Dog.

"Let's roll in the mud."

But Piglet wanted her mama.

"Mama!" said Piglet.

"Your mama's not here," said Horse.

"Let's dance in the daffodils."

But Piglet wanted her mama.

"Mama!" said Piglet.

"Your mama's not here," said Cat.

"Let's snooze in the sun."

But Piglet wanted her mama.

"Oiiiiiink!" cried Piglet.

"Oiiiiiink!
There you are!" said Mama. "I've
been looking everywhere for you."

So with a snuffle and a snort,
Piglet and Mama had a
big pig cuddle.

Then they made
a daisy chain,

played chase,

rolled in the mud,

danced

in

the

daffodils . . .

and snoozed side by side in the sun.